3

JUNIOR

CLASSICS

Published in Red Turtle by
Rupa Publications India Pvt. Ltd 2016
7/16, Ansari Road, Daryaganj
New Delhi 110002

Sales centres:
Allahabad Bengaluru Chennai
Hyderabad Jaipur Kathmandu
Kolkata Mumbai

ISBN: 978-81-291-3887-3

First impression 2016

10 9 8 7 6 5 4 3 2 1

Printed in India by Replika Press Pvt. Ltd.

Contents

The Call of the Wild

Jack London

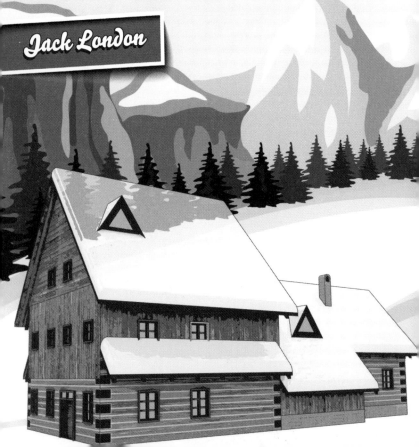

If Buck had read the newspapers, he would have expected trouble.

Buck lived with Judge Miller in a large house surrounded by trees in the sunny Santa Clara Valley. He had ruled over the house, and everything around it, ever since his birth, four years ago.

Buck was the Judge's inseparable companion just like his St Bernard father, Elmo. However, Buck was smaller than Elmo, since his mother, Shep, had been a Scotch shepherd dog. He weighed just 140 pounds, but was well respected, and stayed fit by hunting and swimming.

It was the fall of 1897, and thousands of men were rushing to Canada, searching for gold. And they needed strong dogs, with furry coats that would protect them from the frost. However, Buck did not know any of this.

Manuel, one of the junior gardeners, was fond of gambling but lost often. Unfortunately, Buck did not know that either.

One evening, Manuel led Buck out while the Judge and his boys were away. No one saw them leave. Only one man saw them reach the train station. He handed Manuel some money, and Manuel tied a stout rope around Buck's neck. Buck accepted the rope because he trusted

Manuel, but he growled when the stranger took it. The rope tightened.

He flew at the man, who threw him over. Buck struggled furiously but slowly lost consciousness. Waking up, he found himself in a train's baggage car. His tongue was hurting and he was furious. When the man leapt for him, Buck bit his hand, and the man choked him again.

The next time Buck's eyes opened, he was in a small shed with two men. Dazed and agonized, Buck tried to attack them, but they threw him down and choked him.

Eventually, they flung him into a narrow crate. He lay there, nursing his rage and wounded pride. He was frightened, but did not know why.

The next morning, four evil-looking men came in. They laughed when Buck stormed at them, and put the crate in a wagon.

A few days later, Buck reached Seattle, more furious than ever. He had travelled by wagons, carts, a steamer and a train, and had not eaten or drunk anything in more than forty-eight hours. His throat and tongue were parched and swollen, and his eyes were red.

Four men carried Buck's crate into a high-walled yard, to a stout man in a baggy red sweater. He had a hatchet and a club.

Buck hurled himself against the bars. The man smiled grimly. As he hacked at the crate, Buck rushed at the splintering wood. Soon, the opening was large enough for Buck to get through.

Then the man exchanged the hatchet for the club.

Buck jumped at the man; his hair bristled, his mouth foamed, and his blood-shot eyes glittered madly. Mid-air, Buck received a painful whack, and landed on his side. Buck was confused; he had never been hit before. Again, he launched himself with a snarl. Again, he was knocked down. He now understood the club, but could not stop.

After about a dozen foiled attacks, Buck staggered up again, bleeding profusely. His beautiful coat was flecked with blood and saliva. Then the man hit him on the nose, harder than before. Buck roared in pain, and charged. The man hit him again. Buck crashed to the ground. He rushed one last time. The man struck his hardest blow. Buck collapsed.

When Buck regained consciousness, the man patted his head, and fed and watered him. Thus, Buck learnt to obey a man with a club.

All the dogs that came in met the man in the red sweater and his club. Over a period, men came in and left with one or more dogs. They never came back. Buck wondered where they went. He was scared, and was glad they did not choose him.

Eventually, a little man named Perrault bought Buck and a good-natured Newfoundland called Curly. He handed them over to a giant of a man, called Francois. The men had two more dogs—big and sly Spitz and gloomy Dave—on their ship, which was headed to Canada.

When the ship docked at Dyea, the men leashed the dogs and disembarked. Buck took his first step on land and sprang back in surprise. He had never encountered snow before, and was confused. When he licked the cold white stuff, it felt like fire but disappeared immediately. Confused, he tried it again. Everyone laughed, but Buck felt ashamed.

One day, Curly tried to befriend a large husky dog. He ripped her face open and jumped back quickly. Soon, thirty to forty dogs surrounded the two of them, licking their lips. Curly tried to fight, but kept getting knocked down. When she fell for the last time, the onlookers rushed in and tore her to pieces within two minutes. Buck saw Spitz laughing at Curly, and began to hate him.

Buck realized how savage his new world was, and decided to be always alert.

The next morning, Francois harnessed Buck, Dave and Spitz to a sled. Buck was humiliated—only horses worked at Judge Miller's—but learnt quickly. After his first trip, he knew when to stop and go, and how to turn and run downhill.

One afternoon, Perrault brought in two more huskies—Billee and Joe. They were brothers, but very different: Billee was good-natured, but Joe was nasty. A lean, one-eyed husky called Sol-leks joined them that evening. His name meant 'the angry one', and his battle scars spoke of exceptional skill.

That night Buck learnt that a hole in the snow made a warm nest if he curled up. He fell asleep quickly, but awoke feeling trapped and lost. However, he leapt out of the snow and remembered everything since Manuel's deceit.

Perrault had to deliver urgent dispatches for the Canadian government. So, three more dogs joined the team, and they left.

Dave was wheeler or a sled-dog. Buck was before him and Sol-leks in front of him. The others were strung out ahead, with Spitz in the lead.

The work transformed Dave and Sol-leks. Their lethargy and ill-humour disappeared, and they came alive when they were running. They taught Buck what to do, enforcing their lessons with sharp teeth. Once, during a brief halt, Buck got tangled in the traces and delayed the start. Dave and Sol-leks flew at him. The resulting tangle was even worse, but Buck took care to steer clear of the traces. By the end of the day, Buck had learnt his lessons so well that his companions stopped nagging him. Even Francois did not whip him as much.

That night, they camped at Lake Bennett. Buck fell asleep immediately but woke up exhausted again. The team covered forty miles that day but went slowly where the ice was soft.

Francois guided the sled, while Perrault travelled ahead of the team, packing the snow.

Buck learnt to survive on fish. He also learnt to eat quickly; otherwise, the others would finish their food and steal his. He even learnt to steal food, like his ancestors once did. Still, he was not comfortable in his new world. So, he became cunning and very patient. He did not retaliate even though Spitz constantly bullied him.

One evening, they camped at Lake Le Barge, sheltered by a cliff. Buck's nest beneath the cliff's rock was so snug that he left it, to eat, only reluctantly. When he returned, he found Spitz in his nest. It was a direct threat, so Buck attacked Spitz.

Just then a hundred wild huskies—skinny and mad with hunger—invaded the camp. They targeted the food, and would not leave even when Francois and Perrault hit them.

Then, the huskies turned on the dogs. Three huskies attacked Buck, slashing his head and shoulders, but he fought them off. Dave and Sol-leks were injured but fought bravely. Billee was crying, and Dolly, the last husky added to the team, had a badly torn throat. The team was pushed back towards the cliff. As Buck lunged at his next opponent, Spitz bit into his throat. The huskies retreated for a moment, and Buck shook himself free. However, the savages soon returned, and Buck's team scattered into the nearby forest.

The injured dogs limped back to camp at daybreak. The men were furious: the looters had eaten half the food. In two hours, they packed up, harnessed the dogs and left.

Some of the lakes and rivers had begun to melt and the injured team took six days to cover thirty miles.

Buck's feet were soft, so he suffered tremendously. At the camp, he could not move even to eat, so Francois brought food to him. He also rubbed Buck's feet and made him four little shoes. When Francois forgot the shoes one day, Buck lay down, stuck his legs up in the air and refused to move. Perrault found it hilarious. Buck's feet soon hardened and he stopped using shoes.

One morning, Spitz attacked the weakened Buck, and Francois whipped him. Still, war had been declared between the two dogs.

Spitz feared Buck. Despite being a Southern dog, he had prospered on the trail, thanks to a native sense of cunning. Moreover, Spitz sensed that Buck wanted to become the pack's leader.

Buck's ambition was born from the pride of the trail—the same pride which caused Dave and Sol-leks to lose their innate harshness while running; which inspires dogs to work till they die; and which led Spitz to thrash dogs who shirked. Buck openly threatened Spitz's authority by protecting the shirkers.

Francois knew Buck was guilty of causing trouble, but could not catch him doing it. He kept waiting for the big fight between the main dogs.

In Dawson, Buck saw long teams of working dogs and delightedly joined them in their night-time howling.

Perrault and the team left for Dyea a week later. The dogs were rested, the trail was packed, and there were feeding points along the way. Still, the going was hard.

One night, Dub started chasing a rabbit. The whole team joined him. The rabbit sped down the frozen river. Buck led the dogs along the bank, towards his first kill.

Spitz left the pack and cut across the track. When Buck rounded a bend, he saw Spitz killing the rabbit. Buck flew at Spitz. They rolled over in the snow. Buck was soon bloody and panting but Spitz, a practised fighter, remained untouched.

The fight grew desperate. Buck moved aside at the last moment, and rushed in low. He bit Spitz's left front leg, breaking it. Spitz tried to get up, but Buck kept knocking him down. Eventually, Spitz collapsed for the last time. Buck was the new pack leader.

The next morning, Francois found Spitz missing and Buck injured. He realized what had happened. He predicted that, with Spitz gone, the team would travel much faster.

When Francois led Sol-leks to the lead position, Buck chased him off and took his place. He refused to give up his position even after Francois picked up his club. Finally, Francois threw down his club and Buck took lead position. The men tightened his harness and the team dashed out.

Buck excelled in his new role, and the dogs soon became a team again. When two more huskies—Teek and Koona—joined the team, Buck broke them in very quickly.

The team reached Skaguay after a record run of forty miles a day for fourteen days. A few days later, Perrault and Francois replaced Buck and his team with fresh dogs and disappeared from Buck's life forever.

Buck's team then joined a Scotsman's mail train, the Salt Water Mail train. It was hard work, carrying heavy loads of letters to and from the miners, but Buck performed it well.

At night, he liked stretching out in front of the fire, dreaming his ancestors' dreams about early man.

They were in a hurry and could not rest enough. When they reached Dawson, the dogs were in terrible shape. The weather was awful and the drivers grumbled but they did their best for the dogs.

Dave fell ill. He became unhappy and irritable. The men said something was wrong inside. To allow him to rest, the driver made Sol-leks the sled-dog. However, the pride of the trail was so strong in Dave that he could not bear to see another dog doing his work. Howling mournfully, he followed the sleds and found his team when they stopped.

When it was time to leave, Dave was in his proper place; he had bitten through Sol-lek's traces. The driver realized that Dave wanted to die working, and harnessed him again. Dave pulled proudly, but weakly. The next morning, he could barely stand, but dragged himself to where the team was being harnessed. Then he collapsed.

The drivers led the team behind some trees, and halted. Then the Scotsman went back to the camp. A revolver-shot rang out, and he hurried back. Every single dog knew what had happened.

Thirty days after it left Dawson, the Salt Water Mail reached Skaguay. Having travelled 2,500 miles in less than five months, the dogs were dead tired. Buck had lost twenty-five pounds. Pike and Sol-leks were limping and Dub had a wrenched shoulder blade.

The drivers had expected a long break, but they received orders to sell the worn-out dogs.

and continue on their way with fresh Hudson Bay dogs. So, on their fourth morning in Skaguay, Buck and his mates were bought by two Americans—Hal and Charles.

Charles was a middle-aged man, with weak and watery eyes and a large moustache. Hal was about nineteen or twenty, with a big revolver and a hunting-knife.

Buck realized the Scotsman and the train drivers would disappear, just like Perrault and Francois.

The team soon reached their new owners' camp, where a woman called Mercedes—Hal's sister and Charles' wife—was waiting. The camp was slovenly—tent half-pitched, dishes unwashed, everything in disorder.

Buck watched the men and women uneasily. Their inexperience was obvious. They packed unwashed dishes, rolled up the tent awkwardly and overloaded the sled so much that the dogs could not move it.

Hal whipped them. Mercedes intervened, and some men from a nearby camp pointed out that the dogs were dead tired. However, Hal whipped them again anyway.

The dogs pulled with all their strength but without much success.

One of the onlookers pointed out that the runners were frozen to the ground. This time, the men pushed and the runners broke out. The overloaded sled forged ahead, Buck and his mates struggling frantically.

Buck's new owners had not secured the load properly, and the inexperienced Hal could not control the top-heavy sled. It soon fell over, spilling half its load onto the main street. The dogs kept going, dragging along the lightened sled on its side.

They were angry at being ill-treated, and at the unjust load. Buck broke into a run and the team followed.

Hal tried to stop them, but tripped and fell. The sled went over him. The dogs dashed about, scattering the remainder of the load.

Kind onlookers caught the dogs and gathered up the scattered belongings.

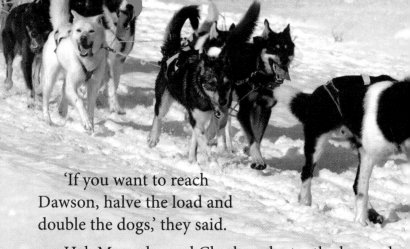

'If you want to reach Dawson, halve the load and double the dogs,' they said.

Hal, Mercedes and Charles reluctantly dumped half their possessions, and bought six more dogs.

The new dogs—three short-haired pointers, one Newfoundland and two mongrels—knew nothing about pulling a sled, and were not interested in learning, despite Buck's efforts.

The dogs were miserable, but the men were cheerful. They did not understand that one sled could not carry enough food for fourteen dogs.

Late next morning, Buck dully led the long team out. Having covered the distance between Salt Water and Dawson four times, he was not happy to be doing it again. None of the dogs was excited. The Outside dogs were frightened and forlorn, and the Insides did not trust their masters, who seemed incapable of learning.

Soon, they had covered only one-fourth the distance, but finished half the dog food. So Hal decreased rations and tried to cover more ground, but failed.

Dub was the first to go. His untreated shoulder blade kept worsening, until finally Hal shot him. Then the six Outsides slowly starved to death.

In their misery, the people fought constantly, ignoring the animals' suffering. Mercedes began riding on the sled, until the animals collapsed. Charles and Hal begged her to get off, but she refused to do so, and threw tantrums.

When the dog food got over, Hal traded his revolver for some frozen horsehide—unhealthy leathery strings covered in indigestible hair.

Buck pulled when he could; when he couldn't, he lay where he fell, until the whip or club made him pull again. His hair was no longer glossy, his muscles had wasted away and his ribs stuck out. The other dogs were also in the same condition.

Soon, Billee and Koona died; and just five dogs—Joe, Pike, Sol-leks, Teek and Buck— were left.

The ice was melting, and thin sections began falling into the river, but neither the humans nor the dogs noticed.

They eventually staggered into John Thornton's camp at the mouth of White River, and the dogs dropped down as if dead. Thornton gave short answers to Hal's questions. Thornton, who was making an axe-handle, warned Hal and Charles not to go ahead.

'The bottom's likely to drop out at any moment,' he said.

Hal sneered, and Thornton, who did not expect his advice to be followed, went back to his work.

When the dogs could not get up, Hal whipped them mercilessly. Slowly and painfully, Sol-leks, Teek, Joe and Pike managed to crawl to their feet. Buck lay where he had fallen. He had sensed impending doom, and had decided to stay put. Thornton's eyes grew moist, and he started pacing. Buck continued to ignore the whipping. Hal then switched to the club. Buck could hear the club hitting his body, but it seemed so far away. He felt strangely numb.

Disgusted by his behaviour, Thornton hurled Hal backwards. He stood over Buck and said, 'If you beat that dog again, I'll kill you.'

'It's my dog,' Hal replied. 'Get out of my way.'

Hal drew his knife but Thornton knocked it onto the floor. When Hal tried to pick it up, Thornton rapped his knuckles. Then he cut Buck's traces.

Hal gave up. Buck was almost dead anyway. Hal led the rest of the staggering team out, with Mercedes perched on the loaded sled.

By the time Thornton finished examining Buck, the sled was a quarter of a mile away. Suddenly, the back end of the sled rose up and the dogs and humans disappeared. The ice had given way.

Thornton's feet had frozen earlier and his partners had left him behind at the camp to recover. He was limping slightly when he rescued Buck, but soon he got better. Slowly, Buck's health improved as well.

Thornton's other companions were a little Irish setter called Skeet and a big black hound called Nig: both amazingly friendly dogs. As Buck grew stronger, Thornton, Skeet and Nig drew him into ridiculous games. And, for the first time, Buck felt love.

Thornton was the ideal master. He treated the dogs as if they were his children. He would take Buck's head between his hands, rest his head upon Buck's and shake him back and forth, muttering soft words. Buck loved this.

For a long time, Buck was afraid Thornton would pass out of his life like the other men had, and so did not let Thornton out of his sight.

Still, Buck had learnt that he must master or be mastered. He retained the wildness he had acquired. He would not steal from Thornton, but everyone else was fair game. He fought fiercely, and soon every dog—except for Skeet and Nig who, apart from being his friends, were off limits because they belonged to Thornton— acknowledged Buck's mastery.

Every day, Buck withdrew more from the world of men. He had heard a sound— mysteriously thrilling—deep in the forest, and it was calling him. When he answered this call, only his love for Thornton drew him back. Other men held no interest. When Thornton's partners—Hans and Pete—returned, Buck tolerated them in a passive sort of way. For Thornton, however, he would do anything.

One day, the men and dogs were sitting at the top of a cliff. Thornton commanded Buck to jump as a joke. Buck almost launched himself off the cliff, and the men had to struggle to drag him back to safety.

A few months later, a man called Black Burton punched Thornton. Buck, who had been lying in a corner and watching his master, roared. He flew up into the air, straight at Burton's throat.

The man instinctively threw out his arm, but fell. Buck let go of the arm, and went for the throat again, tearing it open. Then the crowd drove Buck away while a doctor checked the bleeding. He kept trying to rush to the man, but was forced back. After that, Buck became famous for his loyalty and ferocity.

Buck saved Thornton's life again that autumn.

The three partners were bringing a poling-boat down a bad stretch of rapids. Hans and Pete moved along the bank, steering the boat with a thin rope. Thornton was in the boat, using a pole to help its descent. Buck followed on the bank, his worried eyes never leaving his master.

Hans loosened the rope at a particularly bad spot, and the boat hurtled downstream. Then he tightened the rope too suddenly, and it flipped over. Thornton was thrown into the water and carried downstream towards the worst part of the rapids.

Immediately, Buck jumped in and swam to Thornton. Buck tried to lead Thornton to the bank, but the rapids kept taking them downstream. Thornton scrambled for a handhold among the slippery rocks. When he found one, he released Buck and ordered him to go. Buck took one last look at him and returned to the bank.

Pete and Hans knew that Thornton was in severe danger. They raced up the bank, attached their rope to Buck's neck and shoulders, and tossed him into the stream.

The current made Buck miss Thornton by a few feet. Buck went underwater and remained there. The men hauled him out, and struggled to revive him. Then he heard Thornton's call, and Buck sprang to his feet and ran back up the bank.

The men reattached the rope and Buck jumped in. This time, he swam straight to Thornton. As soon as Thornton held onto Buck's shaggy neck, Hans and Pete pulled them to the bank.

When Thornton regained consciousness, he found that Buck had broken three ribs. The men decided to stay where they were until Buck healed.

One evening that winter, men in the Eldorado Saloon at Dawson were bragging about their favourite dogs. One man said his dog could start a sled with 500 pounds, a second bragged 600 for his dog and a third, 700.

Impulsively, Thornton shouted out that Buck could start a sled with a 1,000 pounds, and walk with it for a hundred yards.

The other men did not believe him. One, named Matthewson, bet a thousand dollars that Buck would fail. Thornton had no idea if Buck would succeed; nor did he have a thousand dollars. But he borrowed the money and placed the bet.

The men streamed out to watch Buck attempt to knock free the sled's frozen runners and pull it for a hundred yards. Thornton began to worry when he saw the loaded sled.

Matthewson offered to bet another thousand, at three to one odds. Thornton, Hans and Pete collected all the money they had—200 dollars—and laid it unhesitatingly against Matthewson's 600.

Buck was excited. The crowd murmured appreciatively at his appearance. He was in perfect condition, his furry coat shone and his mane bristled.

Thornton knelt down, took Buck's head in his hands and whispered, 'As you love me, Buck. As you love me,' and got to his feet. Buck answered by gripping Thornton's hand in his mouth and releasing it slowly.

Buck tightened the traces, and then slacked them several inches.

'Gee!' Thornton's voice rang out. Buck swung to the right, and stopped abruptly. The load quivered, and the ice cracked under the runners.

'Haw!' Thornton commanded. Buck duplicated the move, this time to the left, and the sled broke free.

'Now, mush!'

Buck threw himself forward. He gathered himself compactly, his muscles writhing with the effort.

At first, the sled swayed but stayed put. Slowly, it moved one inch, then another, and another, until it was moving steadily. The crowd cheered as Buck neared the hundred-yard mark. When he passed it, the cheers turned into a roar.

Thornton hugged Buck, and shook him back and forth, muttering his soft loving curses.

Thornton used the 1,600 dollars that Buck earned to pay off his debts and go east. Thornton, Pete and Hans were looking for a fabled lost mine, and would seek their fortunes there. Thornton was unafraid of the wild, and was in no hurry. So they hunted, and fished and lived off the land in a leisurely manner, to Buck's endless delight.

They spent a whole year wandering around in search of the prized mine. It was spring again when they came upon a valley, where the gold shone like yellow butter across the bottom of the washing-pan. They stopped there.

The men worked every day, collecting gold dust and nuggets worth thousands of dollars and storing it in moose-hide bags.

The dogs had nothing to do, except hauling in the meat that Thornton killed now and again, and Buck spent long hours musing by the fire. He often had visions of early man—the memories of his ancestors—and sometimes walked with him in the dream world.

With the visions came the call from deep within the forest, filling him with strange desires. Sometimes, he followed the call into the forest, smelling the earth smells and exploring the fungus-covered trunks of fallen trees, wide-eyed and wide-eared.

Irresistible impulses seized him. He would be dozing lazily in camp, when suddenly his head would snap up, and he would spring to his feet and dash away. He spent hours and days running through the forest and down dry watercourses and creeping upon the birds.

One night, the call came: a long-drawn howl, similar to, yet unlike any noise made by a husky. Buck dashed through the sleeping camp and headed for the forest. In a clearing, he saw—erect on haunches—with nose pointed to the sky, a long lean timber wolf.

He sensed Buck's presence and ceased his howling. Buck stalked into the open in that peculiar manner—half-menacing, half-friendly—that marks the meeting of wild beasts. The wolf fled.

Buck followed, and chased the wolf into a blind channel. The cornered wolf became defensive, and snapped his teeth. Buck did not attack, but circled the wolf making friendly advances. The wolf was suspicious and afraid for Buck was thrice as big as him. He kept running away, but eventually, Buck's persistence paid off. The wolf, finding that no harm was intended, finally sniffed noses with him. Once they became friendly, the wolf started off at an easy pace, and indicated that Buck was to go with him. They ran side by side for many hours through great stretches of forest and many streams. Buck was wildly glad. He was finally answering the call. Old memories were coming back to him: he had done this before, somewhere in that other and dimly remembered world.

They stopped by a stream to drink, and Buck remembered Thornton. He sat down. The wolf started to go on, then returned to Buck, encouraging him to accompany him. But Buck turned about and ran back to the camp.

Rushing in, Buck affectionately knocked Thornton down and licked his face. Thornton responded by shaking Buck's head and cursing him lovingly.

Buck stayed at camp for two days and nights, never letting Thornton out of his sight. But then, the call sounded more demanding than ever. Buck's restlessness returned, and he was haunted by recollections of the wild brother. He wandered the woods again, but the wild brother did not come; and though he listened carefully, the mournful howl was never raised.

Buck was becoming even wilder. He was a survivor in a hostile environment and he was proud of it. He looked like a gigantic wolf except for the stray brown on his muzzle and above his eyes and the splash of white hair that ran down the middle of his chest.

He hunted as he travelled and fished for salmon. Once, he even killed a large black bear that was blinded by mosquitoes while it was fishing.

One day, a band of twenty moose appeared in the fall, and Buck enjoyed the challenge they posed. Buck managed to cut the bull out from the herd. He was six feet high with large foot antlers—a worthy opponent. Buck stalked him for four days, and killed him. It was not easy.

For a day and a night, Buck stayed near his kill, eating and sleeping. Then, refreshed, he turned towards the camp.

As he went closer, he sensed a calamity. Neck hair bristling, Buck hurried on.

Three miles away he found a new trail and followed it into a thicket. Nig was lying on his side, dead where he had dragged himself, an arrow protruding from either side of his body.

A hundred yards farther on, Buck came upon one of

the sled-dogs, which Thornton had bought in Dawson, in its death throes. Buck did not stop. From the camp came the faint sound of voices. Creeping forward, Buck found Hans, lying on his face, feathered with arrows. Buck peered out and let out a ferocious growl.

The Yeehats tribespeople, the region's fearsome buffalo hunters, were dancing about the wreckage of the spruce-bough lodge when they heard a fearful roaring. Rushing upon them was an animal the like of which they had never seen before. It was Buck—hurling himself upon them in a frenzy to destroy. He sprang at the foremost man, ripping his throat wide open. Buck kept going, tearing and destroying, in constant and terrific motion.

The Yeehats fled in terror to the woods, mistaking Buck for an Evil Spirit.

Buck raged at their heels and hunted them. Finally, Buck returned to the camp. He found Pete in his blankets, killed in the first moment of surprise. Buck followed Thornton's desperate struggle down to the edge of a deep pool. By the edge, lay Skeet, faithful to the last. His scent told Buck that Thornton lay dead in the pool.

Thornton's death left a great void in Buck—a void which ached and ached. Occasionally, he would look at the Yeehat carcasses and feel proud.

He had killed a man under the law of club and fang. And they had died so easily. Buck would never fear humans, except when armed. With Thornton dead, man and the claims of man no longer bound him. He was finally ready to obey the call of the wild.

Soon, the wolf pack poured into Buck's valley. Buck stood motionless at the centre of the clearing. They were awed by him at first, but soon the boldest one attacked. In a flash, Buck broke his neck. Then he stood, as still as before. Three others attacked but soon retreated, blood streaming from slashed throats or shoulders.

Then the whole pack surged forward, eager to bring Buck down. However, Buck was too quick for them.

To prevent them from getting behind him, he retreated to a right angle in a high gravel bank. In half an hour, wolves drew back. They were all watching Buck or lapping water from the pool, when one wolf, long and lean and grey, advanced cautiously, in a friendly manner. Buck recognized the wild brother. He was whining softly, and, as Buck whined, they touched noses.

Then an old battle-scarred wolf came forward. Buck began to snarl but sniffed noses with him. The old wolf sat down, pointed his nose at the moon and howled. The others sat down and howled. Buck, too, sat down and howled. He came out of his angle and the pack crowded around him, sniffing. Then the pack sprang into the woods, and Buck ran with them, side by side with the wild brothers.

A few years later, the Yeehats noticed that some timber wolves had splashes of brown on head and muzzle with a rift of white centring down the chest. They also tell the tale of a fearsome Ghost Dog that leads the pack.

Sometimes, missing hunters are found with slashed throats and surrounded by wolf prints—larger than any wolf—in the snow.

There is one valley the Yeehats never enter, even when following the moose, for it is haunted by an Evil Spirit. However, every summer, one visitor goes there: a great wolf. He stands in an open space among the trees for a while, howls long and mournfully once, and departs.

However, he is not always alone. When the wolves hunt, he may be seen leading the pack, howling out the song of the pack.

Moby Dick
or
The Whale

Herman Melville

Call me Ishmael. Some years ago, being penniless and bored, I decided to join a whaling crew. Going to sea would cure my boredom, being paid to work would cure my poverty and, having worked on merchant ships before, whaling would be a new experience as well.

In those days, I thought I was making a choice; I can now see it was destiny. I still do not know why the fate chose me but, over a period of time, I can see exactly how I was reeled in. First, I was curious about the great whale itself and thought it would be an adventure to face the mysterious monster. The added chance of travelling to exotic lands cemented my participation.

I stuffed some clothes in a bag and left Manhatto. While New Bedford is now a hub for whalers, Nantucket was the first. So I was bent on joining a Nantucket craft. When I reached New Bedford, the Nantucket-bound boat had already sailed.

With the next boat not due to sail until three days later, I set out to find cheap accommodation. After hours of searching, I found the Spouter Inn, run by Peter Coffin.

There were no spare rooms, so I would have to share the room with a dark-skinned harpooner. During dinner, I decided to sleep on the dining room bench rather than share a stranger's bed. The bench was very uncomfortable. Soon, it was midnight, and the mysterious harpooner had not returned. So I took the landlord's offer, and headed to the room. It was small and cold, with a big uncomfortable bed.

I had just fallen asleep when the harpooner returned. His appearance terrified me. His face was purplish yellow, with large black tattoos. His head was bald, except for a small knot of hair near his forehead.

Then, he took out a stumpy idol, prayed to it before putting it back in a bag.

Then he lit a pipe and climbed into bed. I let out a little cry, and he finally noticed that I was in the room.

He thought I was a devil, and threatened to kill me. The noise brought the landlord to the room. I jumped off the bed and ran to him.

'Don't be afraid, Queequeg would not hurt you at all,' the landlord said, grinning.

'Stop grinning! Why did you not tell me he was a cannibal?' I asked, for that is what he was.

'I thought you would figure it out. Did not I tell you he was selling heads?' He turned to Queequeg and told him about the sleeping arrangements.

Queequeg nodded, and told me to get back into bed.

'I won't touch you,' he said, charitably.

For a cannibal, he seemed nice enough. So I asked him to put away his pipe, which he did, and I climbed back into bed, said goodnight to the landlord and fell fast asleep.

Queequeg was hugging me when I awoke. I could not move. When I finally managed to wake him up, he looked confused for a while, but then seemed to remember the previous night's events.

Queequeg signalled I could dress after he had left. It was a very civilized gesture. I reciprocated by staring at him rudely as he put on his hat and boots before he put on his clothes. Then, he shaved with his harpoon, put on his heavy monkey jacket and went out, carrying his harpoon.

I quickly followed suit, and saw Queequeg using his harpoon to spear the rare steaks he ate. Breakfast done, I went out for a stroll, and found that Queequeg was not the strangest thing about New Bedford.

Most people were sailors, but I also saw cannibals standing about chatting on the streets; some were even carrying around human flesh.

I visited the town's little chapel, as seamen always do on Sundays before a voyage. The chapel and the pulpit seemed to stand testament to the chaplains' years as a whaler. As I sat contemplating human mortality, I was surprised to find Queequeg there despite the raging storm.

Soon, the popular old chaplain Father Mapple approached the pulpit. He asked the people to gather in the front. He started with a prayer. Next, he began reading a hymn, but started singing it towards the middle. Almost everyone sang along.

Then, Father Mapple gave a sermon about a man called Jonah. Jonah had disobeyed God and was running away to sea to escape punishment. He repented after being swallowed by a whale, and God rescued him. Sermon done, the priest knelt down and prayed silently until everyone left.

I returned to the inn, and saw Queequeg, sitting by the fire. At my arrival, he took out a book and began counting the pages, in batches of fifty. I did not think he could count any higher. I realized that beneath all his strange markings lay an honest heart and a noble soul. I decided to befriend him. Queequeg and I had become good friends by the time we went up to our room. He presented me with an embalmed head and fifteen silver dollars. Then, he took out his idol and got ready to pray. He was eager that I join him, so I did.

We chatted for a while, and went to sleep.

I later learnt that Queequeg was a tribal prince from Rokovoko, who had always wanted to see the world. He had tried to get a job on a visiting ship, but the captain turned him down. So, he paddled out to sea and jumped onto the ship's deck and refused to move even when threatened by the captain of the ship. Eventually the captain relented, and the savage learnt to be a harpooner.

His father had been old when Queequeg had left home, and he also told me that he would be crowned king when he returned. Yet, Queequeg wanted to return to the sea. So, on Monday, we boarded *The Moss* together to sail to Nantucket.

We were so excited to be on water that we did

not notice people staring at us. When Queequeg caught a youngster making fun of him behind his back, he picked him up and threw him into the air. The youngster landed on his feet and ran, complaining to the captain.

The captain was shocked when Queequeg explained that the youngster was too unimportant to be killed. He threatened to harm Queequeg if the harpooner misbehaved.

Soon after, the lad was swept overboard, and Queequeg rescued him single-handedly, earning the respect of crew and passengers alike.

We anchored in Nantucket that evening and went to the Try Pots—an inn run by Coffin's cousin Hosea Hussey—where we devoured steaming pots of clam and cod-chowder. We were on the way to our room, when Mrs Hussey stepped forward. She explained that she did not allow weapons in the rooms ever since a guest accidentally harpooned himself. So she took Queequeg's harpoon and noted down our breakfast order.

The next day was some sort of a holy day for Queequeg. So, he stayed shut up with Yojo, his little wooden idol. As instructed by Yojo, via Queequeg, I set out to find us a ship and found the *Pequod*, which was named after an extinct tribe of Massachusetts Indians. The small old ship looked cannibalized as it was made up of bits from all over the world. Her owner, Captain Peleg, had also added the bones and teeth of Sperm Whales— trophies collected over fifty years in the business.

I met Captain Peleg aboard the *Pequod*. He told me how the ship's Captain Ahab had lost one of his legs to a great whale, interviewed me and introduced me to one of his colleagues Captain Bildad.

Instead of wages, whalers were given a share of the profits—which were called lays—based on their ability and responsibility. They offered me about three hundredth lay—much less than I had expected even as a newcomer to the industry. Still, I agreed, and told them about Queequeg. They told me to bring him along the next day.

When I asked about the reclusive Captain Ahab, the men said he was 'a grand, ungodly, god-like man'. He seemed destined to follow in the path of the evil king he was named after, they said. However, he had a young wife and an infant son, so there must be some good in him, they added.

I left, thinking about the captain and in awe of him.

Queequeg's Ramadan lasted till dawn the next morning. Until then, he just sat on the floor, as still as Yojo, and ignored everyone around him.

As dawn broke, he got up and stretched. We ate hearty chowder breakfasts and walked along to the *Pequod*.

Queequeg proved himself by hitting a small speck of tar in the water, and captains Peleg and Bildad offered him ninetieth lay. Then we left, but were stopped by a ragged man named Elijah. When we said we had signed onto the *Pequod*, he rambled about how dangerous Ahab was and how we deserved to sail with him. Then, he wandered off.

The next few days went in a flurry of activity as the *Pequod* prepared to sail.

When the day came, we boarded the vessel and learnt that Captain Ahab was already onboard. Soon, the deck was bustling with last-minute preparations. Captain Ahab remained in his cabin.

Around noon on Christmas, we weighed anchor and set the sails, and the captain was still in his cabin. The retired captains, Pelag and Bildad, left the ship reluctantly, jumping onto the pilot boat just as it was leaving. At last we plunged into the Atlantic.

The crew was hardworking and diverse. The chief mate of the ship, Starbuck, was a thin man from Nantucket. He firmly believed that courage came from knowing danger and overcoming one's fears. Stubb, the happy-go-lucky second mate, came from Cape Cod. To him, courage was a practical skill. The third mate was Flask, a short stout fellow from Tisbury who believed that whales existed to be killed. In a hunt, each of these mates would work in tandem with a harpooner: Queequeg with Starbuck, Tashtego with Stubb and Daggoo with Flask.

Captain Ahab emerged once we hit warm weather. His whale-bone leg shone in the sun.

The *Pequod* gradually sailed into regions where spring seemed eternal. Ahab did not sleep more than three hours a night, and spent most of his waking hours in the open air.

One morning, the captain told us to watch out for a white whale.

Some days later, he nailed a Spanish gold coin to the main mast, and promised to give it to the first man who spotted the white whale. Tashtego, Daggoo and Queequeg had all seen this whale— Moby Dick—which had taken Ahab's leg. It had outrun whalers for years and so many harpoons were stuck on him that he looked like a pincushion.

Captain Ahab wanted to take revenge. Besides, he believed the whale symbolized everything that was evil. Everyone was excited about the hunt except

Starbuck. He felt Moby Dick would not fetch much money and, moreover, should not be punished because of someone's whim. But Ahab was adamant.

Moby Dick was legendary. Not many people had seen him, but almost everyone had heard stories of the unusually large whale which had destroyed its pursuers and then escaped. Sailors were frightened of his gigantic size, unusual appearance and, most of all, his destructive intelligence.

The idea of Moby Dick filled me with unknown dread. Its unnatural whiteness made it worse. White was a colour generally associated with virtue but, here, like a phantom, it seemed to foretell disaster.

Ahab had been obsessed with the whale since it took his leg on his previous voyage. He also knew that the men would eventually mutiny if they did not have something to hold on to. So he promised them cash.

One night, Dough-Boy, one of the men on watch, heard a strange noise. He was convinced there were people on board who had not been seen yet, but his colleagues thought he was imagining things.

Time passed. One day, Tashtego spotted a school of Sperm Whales. Suddenly, five strangers appeared alongside Ahab. He had smuggled them on board as his private harpoon crew.

Led by a tall turbaned man named Fedallah, they quickly untied one of the boats. Ahab ordered us to lower the boats. Soon, the *Pequod's* four boats—headed by Ahab, Starbuck, Stubb and Flask—were in the water, spread out, so as to cover the maximum area.

I was in Starbuck's boat, and we were following three whales. That evening, on Starbuck's direction, Queequeg's harpoon flew out towards a great hump. The boat pitched, and the crew was tossed into the water. The whale had escaped with just a scratch.

We climbed back into the boat. It was full of water though largely unharmed. So, we tied our oars together to form a floatation device, and sat waiting, until the *Pequod* picked us up the next morning.

When I got back onto the deck, I decided to update my will.

The crew was worried that—considering how important the captain's well-being was to the voyage—he was needlessly risking his life by actively participating in the hunt, especially with his bad leg.

The five additional men soon found a place in the crew, but Fedallah remained a mystery.

One night, Fedallah saw a glimmer of a whale, but it soon disappeared. It appeared and disappeared as the weeks passed, leading us on like a phantom guide. The men swore it was Moby Dick.

Eventually, Captain Ahab took us around the Cape of Good Hope and further into the stormy Indian Ocean.

We came upon the ghostlike *Goney* or *Albatross*. Ahab asked the crew if they had seen Moby Dick. Just as he was about to answer, the other captain dropped his speaking trumpet and could not be heard over the high winds. The men considered this an omen.

Ahab declared we would be sailing around the world.

As the ships' wakes crossed, the shoals of little fish, which had been swimming alongside us, changed course and began following the *Goney*—this was another omen. Our captain, however, did not believe in omens.

Normally, when two or more whaling ships met on the ocean, it was customary to exchange visits, news, reading materials and letters. Such visits were called 'gams.' But Ahab was not interested in ships that did not carry news of the white whale.

One such gam took place with a whaler called the *Town-Ho*. According to Steelkilt, one of the *Town-Ho*'s sailors, he led the other sailors in a mutiny after being mistreated by Radney—one of the mates. However, the mutiny failed and the mutineers were captured and flogged by Radney. They were released later. Steelkilt was very angry that Radney flogged him even though the captain did not. So he planned to murder Radney.

Before the murder, however, the ship saw Moby Dick. When Radney tried to harpoon the whale, he fell into the water and the beast caught him in his jaws. When we saw her, the *Town-Ho* was battered and looked like she had been pierced by swordfish. When I told this story to a friend in Lima, they would not believe me. However, having met and spoken to Steelkilt, I could swear that it was true.

Most whale pictures are inaccurate, and I feel the only way to get an accurate picture is to see it up close. But that is a dangerous undertaking. The only two accurate images of whales I know are French engravings—this is ironic, since France is not a whaling nation.

Making our way through meadows of brit—the minute yellow substance whales feed on—we continued towards Java.

One morning, Daggoo saw what he thought was a white whale. We lowered the boats and chased it. However, it turned out to be a giant squid. The superstitious whalers considered this a bad omen, but Queequeg predicted that we would soon catch a whale. He was proven right the next day, when Stubb and Tashtego killed a spouting Sperm Whale. We spent the day hauling the carcass back to the *Pequod*.

Most whalers do not eat whale meat, but Stubb wanted a whale steak for dinner. While he gorged on his steak, sharks attacked the rest of the whale. Stubb demanded that the cook order the sharks to stay away from his whale. In turn, the cook lectured the sharks on good manners. He started off politely.

'Fellow creatures, I've been ordered to say that you must stop that noise. Stop that smacking of the lips! Master Stubb says you can fill your bellies, but you must stop that racket.'

When they would not stop the noise, he tried another trick. He appealed to them to 'govern their voracious appetites' and to 'be civil' while eating the whale.

'Don't tear out the blubber from your neighbour's mouth,' he said. 'I know some of you have very big mouths, bigger than the others; but then big mouths sometimes have small bellies. So the bigness of the mouth is not to swallow with, but to bite off the blubber for the small sharks, that cannot help themselves.'

Eventually, he gave up.

'Cursed creatures! Make as much noise as you can! Fill your bellies, and die!' he yelled at them.

Then, when they refused to go, we beat them. Queequeg nearly cut off his hand on a dead shark's sharp teeth.

The next day, we harvested the whale's skin, peeling it off like an orange rind. The Sperm Whale's head contains spermaceti, which is used to make lamp oil. So we cut off its head and then dropped the rest of the carcass into the sea, where the vultures and sharks would feast on it.

We soon met the *Jeroboam*, and Captain Mayhew brought a boat alongside to talk to Ahab. Stubb identified one of the men as a former prophet who called himself the archangel Gabriel. Captain Mayhew tried to tell Ahab a story about the white whale but Gabriel kept interrupting. He said the whale was an incarnation of God, and that anyone who hunted it would be killed.

Some days later, we killed a Right Whale. Stubb asked Flask what they should do with it, since Right Whales are not very valuable. Flask answered that according to Fedallah a ship carrying a Right Whale's head and a Sperm Whale's head would never capsize. Fedallah stood so close to Ahab that their shadows seemed to merge and grow. Most of the men thought he was evil.

Near Indonesia, we sighted a great herd of Sperm Whales.

This was unusual, since Sperm Whales are generally seen in smaller groups called schools. Some of these are made up entirely of male 'bulls'. Others comprise a 'harem' of females and young ones—'cows' and 'calves'—and a single bull known as the lord. Whalers only target cows and calves, since bulls are too large and dangerous.

We were preparing to lower the boats when Tashtego noticed a pirate ship chasing us. We outran them and turned our attention back to the whales.

The whales were no longer in a line. They were circling in a panicked ring.

Soon, we were trying to separate one of them from the herd. Within three minutes, Queequeg's harpoon had wounded one of the giants. It let out a massive spray of water and tried to escape— dragging us straight through the water.

Queequeg steered us out of the dangerous herd. We speared two more whales with druggs— two thick squares of wood clamped together and attached to a harpoon with a long rope. Whalers use these heavy devices to exhaust the whale of its energy, slowing it down to kill it at their convenience.

We slid into the centre of the whale circle. It was calm at first, but after a while the whales converged on the centre. We barely made it out, and Queequeg lost his hat in the effort. By the end of the day, we had killed only one whale.

When one of Stubb's oarsmen sprained his hand, Pip—the cabin boy—was recruited to replace him.

On his second trip, a harpooned whale nudged the boat. Startled, the boy fell out and got tangled up in the ropes. The men had to cut him free. Stubb warned Pip that if he ever jumped out again he would not be rescued. However, Pip fell in again. So Stubb left him in the water for a few hours. When Stubb eventually rescued the boy, he began to speak without making much sense. The men said he had gone mad, but I had a feeling he had gained prophetic wisdom.

We later met the *Samuel Enderby*, whose captain, Boomer, lost his arm to Moby Dick. The two captains touched their false limbs in greeting. As the evening progressed, Boomer said he had seen the whale again, but refused to hunt it. He also refused to tell Ahab which way it was headed. Ahab left angrily.

Ahab stepped onto the boat so hard, his ivory leg cracked. So he ordered the carpenter to make him another, stronger, one.

The next time the men pumped the water out of the hold, they found that some oil casks were leaking. Starbuck asked Ahab if they could stop to fix them. Ahab refused and they started arguing. When Ahab pointed a musket at him, Starbuck warned Ahab to be careful and walked away. Ahab considered his words, and ordered us to fix the leaking casks. I think he did it to avoid making the men angry.

During this time, Queequeg fell very ill and thought he was going to die. So he ordered a coffin to be made, filled it with all his personal possessions, lied down in it and waited to die. Pip danced around him. Soon, Queequeg felt better and used the coffin for storage.

Ahab wanted a special harpoon which he could use to kill Moby Dick. He gave the blacksmith some nails from shoes of racehorses, which is the toughest steel known to man, and began to give him instructions. However, he soon took over, and used blood to temper the iron.

A few weeks after Ahab's harpoon was ready, the *Pequod* came across the *Bachelor*, a Nantucket whaler returning home after a successful voyage. It was cheerfully decorated—with signals, ensigns and jacks of all colours on every side—and the men wore red streamers in their hats. They had been so successful that they had bartered food for empty casks in which to store their catch. The thrilled whalers were having a party.

As the two ships passed each other, Ahab asked the other captain if he had seen the white whale. He said he had only heard of Moby Dick, but did not believe he existed. He invited Ahab to join the party, but Ahab refused and the two vessels went their own way.

The next day, we bagged four whales. One of them died quite a distance from the ship. So we could not take it back that day. Ahab and Fedallah were on the boat sent out to keep watch. Soon, they were the only ones awake.

Ahab had been dreaming about dying, but Fedallah told him, 'You will not die until you have seen two hearses, one not made by mortal hands and one made of wood from America.'

This calmed Ahab, since they were unlikely to find hearses—vehicles that carry corpses—at sea.

'Besides,' Fedallah continued, 'Only hemp can kill you.'

This convinced Ahab that he would probably be hanged and that was also unlikely to happen at sea.

When a typhoon struck the next day the *Pequod*'s three masts lit up like spermaceti candles. The crew was worried about a lightning strike, but Ahab refused to let them put up lightning rods.

Ahab saw the white flames as signs of his own power. Starbuck disagreed with him. When Ahab's harpoon lit up, he took it as a sign that God opposed Ahab's ambition. Ahab, however, held out the harpoon in front of the frightened crew, declared that there was nothing to fear and then blew out 'the last fear'.

When Starbuck asked Ahab if they should take down the sails to avoid danger, the captain insisted that the men just tie them tighter together. Later, when Stubb and Flask were discussing Ahab's hazardous behaviour, Stubb pointed out that their journey was no more dangerous than any other.

The storm finally calmed down. When Starbuck went down to report to Ahab, he passed a row of muskets, including the one Ahab had used to threaten him. Starbuck—who was angry at Ahab—seriously considered killing the sleeping captain, but then decided not to.

The next day, Ahab realized the storm had ruined his compass, and made a new needle. When he saw that none of his other navigational instruments were working, he asked Pip to help, but Pip responded with nonsense.

'Pip? Who's Pip? Pip jumped from the whale-boat. Pip's missing. I guess he's holding on. Ho! There's his arm just breaking water. Captain Ahab! sir, sir! Here's Pip, trying to get on board again,' Pip said.

Ahab heard his rant and asked him, 'Who are you, boy?'

'Bell-boy, sir; ship's-crier; ding, dong, ding! Pip! Pip! Pip! One hundred pounds of clay reward for Pip; five feet high—looks cowardly—quickest known by that! Ding, dong, ding! Who's seen Pip the coward?' Pip answered.

Ahab then announced that he was giving the boy his cabin, since the 'luckless child' had touched his 'inmost centre'.

One night, the men thought they heard mermaids wailing or perhaps they were ghosts. They were terrified but Ahab laughed and explained that they had passed a seal colony. This did not comfort the whalers, who thought seals were unlucky. The next morning, one of the men fell overboard. The old lifebuoy leaked and sank, taking the man with it. Starbuck, Stubb and Flask decided to replace the lifebuoy with Queequeg's coffin.

Later, we met Captain Gardiner's *Rachel*. Gardiner's son had been lost while they were hunting Moby Dick but, in his eagerness to pursue the whale, Ahab refused to help look for the boy.

Now that we knew Moby Dick was near, Ahab paced the deck constantly. Pip tried to accompany him, promising never to leave him. Ahab told the boy to stay in the cabin since his sympathy for the insane Pip might distract him from the hunt. Fedallah, however, continued to shadow Ahab.

The crew grew more uneasy as Ahab's obsession intensified. He wanted to be the first one to sight the whale. So Starbuck helped him to climb on to the main mast. He stood there, watching the sea, when a large black hawk swooped down and carried his hat away. It was another bad omen.

We next met the *Delight*. She had met the white whale, and had been badly damaged in the encounter. Many men had also died. The *Delight*'s crew considered the *Pequod*'s coffin-lifebuoy hanging at its stern a bad sign.

One pleasant morning, Ahab was pacing the deck when he met Starbuck. Starbuck and the captain started chatting about life in general and their wives. Ahab called himself a fool for chasing Moby Dick. When Starbuck suggested that he call off the hunt, Ahab said he could not because it was his destiny. Starbuck left in despair.

That night, Ahab announced he could smell Moby Dick nearby. He climbed onto the mast. He soon spotted the whale—finally after a long time—and earned himself the gold coin nailed to the mast. We lowered the boats at once but the whale was underwater. When he finally surfaced, he came up from directly beneath Ahab's boat, teeth shining in massive jaws. The boat broke and the men were thrown out into the water. The giant whale rushed at the men but, luckily, Starbuck had seen the scene from the *Pequod*. He quickly brought the ship and chased the whale away. The other boats rescued the men from the water.

The whale swam quickly, and Starbuck and the men uneasily kept watch all night. At dawn, the chase intensified. They saw Moby Dick and lowered the boats. Starbuck stayed with the *Pequod*.

This time, Ahab decided to attack Moby Dick head-on. They managed to spear him with a harpoon, but he got away. They attacked him again, and he manoeuvred this way and that, until he caused the boats carrying Flask and Stubb to crash into each other. Many of the men got tangled in the harpoons and lances. Ahab cut the tangle and reattached the single harpoon, but the whale capsized his boat, breaking Ahab's whale-bone leg in the process.

Ahab returned to the *Pequod*. The men told him how the tangled lines had pulled Fedallah into the ocean and drowned him. He realized that one part of Fedallah's prophecy had come true. He had died before Ahab. Again, Starbuck begged Ahab to call off the hunt, but he refused.

The carpenter quickly made Ahab a replacement leg from the debris of his harpoon boat.

On the third day, we looked for the whale, but did not see him. The air was fraught with tension. Around noon, Ahab climbed to the top of the mast and saw Moby Dick following us. The whale was dragging along the harpoons we had pierced him with over the past two days.

We turned the ship around. Ahab came back on deck and shook hands with Starbuck before we lowered the boats. Starbuck was in charge now. Sharks nipped at our oars as we headed towards

Moby Dick. When he surfaced, he damaged two boats, leaving only Ahab's boat intact.

The previous day's tangled lines had bound Fedallah's corpse to the whale. When Ahab saw this, he saw this was the first hearse from Fedallah's prediction—the one not made by mortal hands.

Ahab sent the other men back to the ship, and looked for the whale. It had been swimming under water and now came up near the ship. Ahab followed quickly and, when he came near the ship, heard Starbuck calling for him to desist from his madness.

The sharks swam alongside Ahab's boat and kept crunching off bits of the oars.

Suddenly, Moby Dick changed course and headed straight for the *Pequod*. Ahab gave chase, hoping to save his ship. Tashtego was trying to hammer a new flag into place. Ahab, Starbuck and Stubb all sighted the monstrous whale at the same time.

'The second hearse!' Ahab said, for the ship was made from American wood and would entomb his whole crew.

Angry, Ahab struck at the whale with all his might. The injured whale darted forward and the rope tied to the harpoon got stuck in the grooves of the oars.

Ahab ducked to avoid it. However, the hemp line wrapped around his neck like a gallows rope and dragged him overboard—just as Fedallah had prophesied. It was over in a flash. The men had not even realized what had happened.

Then, the whale slammed into the ship. With an explosive crack, it broke in half and began to sink.

Soon, only the uppermost masts were visible. A little while later, even those had been swallowed into the sea. The whirlpool created by the sinking ship pulled the other harpoon boats and their crew into the water.

I escaped, but only because I had been thrown clear when Ahab's boat was destroyed and watched the entire scene from the sidelines. I was drawn in, slowly, by the vortex. It subsided just as I reached the centre, and Queequeg's coffin shot out to the surface and floated near me. I used it as a lifebuoy for almost two days before *Rachel* picked me up. Still searching for his lost son, Captain Gardiner had found another orphan.

The Little Mermaid

Hans Christian Andersen

Far out into the ocean, where the water was bluer and deeper than you can imagine, lived the Sea King and his subjects. Life existed in the Sea Kingdom at the bottom of the ocean—plants and flowers and fishes like birds. In the deepest part was located the castle of the Sea King, with walls of coral and high windows of clearest amber. The roof was made of oysters, each of which opened and closed as the water flew over them to reveal a glittering pearl. In calm weather, the sun shone through like a purple flower.

The Sea King's wife died many years ago, but his mother took care of the castle and the six sea-princesses. They were all beautiful but the youngest was the prettiest. She had clear delicate skin and eyes as blue as the deepest sea; but like her sisters, she had no feet. Her body ended in a fish's tail.

The princesses played in the castle halls or among the flowers that grew out of the walls or with the fish that swam in through the open windows. Bright red and dark blue flowers grew in the cobalt blue sand of the garden outside the castle. Each princess had her own little flowerbed in the garden, to arrange into any shape she wanted. The youngest sea-princess made hers round, with flowers as red as the setting sun.

She also had a statue of a young prince, which had drifted down from a wreck.

She was a quiet child. While her sisters delighted in treasures they found on the shipwreck, she loved to listen to her grandmother's stories about the world above the sea—stories of ships and towns, and people and animals.

'When you are eighteen,' the grandmother said one day, 'you will be allowed to rise up to the surface of the sea, to sit on the rocks in the moonlight, watching the ships sailing by. Then, you will see both forests and towns.'

The oldest sea-princess would turn eighteen that year, but since each sister was a year younger than the other the youngest could not see our world for another five years. Each promised to tell the others what she saw on her first visit, since not even the wise old grandmother could give them all the information they wanted. The youngest princess waited patiently for her turn. Often, she stood by the open window at night, watching the fish swimming through the dark blue water. When a black shadow passed, she knew it was either a whale, or a ship full of humans who never imagined that a little mermaid was looking up at them from beneath.

When the oldest sister returned from her first trip to the surface, she talked about a hundred things; but the most beautiful, she said, was to lie on a sandbank in the moonlight and watch the lights in the nearby city, twinkling like hundreds of stars, and to listen to the noise of carriages and the voices of human beings. However, because she could not experience any of that, the youngest princess longed for them more than ever, and thought about the great city when she stood at her window at night.

The second sister gushed about the sunset when she returned from the surface. The whole sky looked gold, she said, with violet and deep pink clouds. She swam towards the sun but it sunk into the waves, and the rosy tints faded from the clouds and from the sea.

The third sister swam up a broad river. On the banks, she saw green hills, palaces and castles, and she heard the birds singing. To her, the rays of the sun were so powerful that she had to dive down under the water to cool off. She wanted to join the group of human children she found playing in a narrow creek, but they fled in fear as soon as they saw her. Later, a dog came to the water and barked at her. She did not know what it was but got frightened and rushed back home. However, she said she should never forget the beautiful forest, the green hills and the pretty children who could swim even without fish's tails.

The fourth sister said her favourite part was the sky, which looked like a bell of glass. She also spoke of the whales, which spouted water from their nostrils until they resembled a hundred fountains.

The fifth sister was born in winter, so when she went up, she saw something that none of her sisters had seen. The sea was green and large icebergs were floating about glittering like diamonds. Those were larger than anything she had ever seen. She sat on one of them and let the wind play with her long hair. She noticed that ships sailed by rapidly, steering far away from the iceberg. In the evening, dark clouds covered the sky and the setting sun glowed red on the icebergs. People on the ships were terrified, but she sat calmly on the iceberg, watching the blue lightning flashing into the sea.

Now that they could swim wherever they pleased, the older sisters soon became indifferent towards life on land and preferred to spend their time at home. Yet, often in the evenings, the five sisters would rise to the surface in a row.

In stormy weather, the mermaids swam near ships that were in danger of sinking and sang sweetly of the Sea Kingdom's delights, begging sailors not to be afraid of sinking to the bottom. However, the sailors could not understand the song and were afraid of it.

Through all this, the youngest sea-princess looked on, ready to cry, but suffering more since mermaids have no tears.

'If only I were eighteen years old! I know I will love everything, and everyone, up there!' she said.

Finally, on her eighteenth birthday, her grandmother

placed a wreath of white lilies in her hair and
ordered eight oysters to attach themselves to her
tail to show her high rank. The princess did not
like the painful oysters and would have preferred
a wreath of her own red flowers but she could
not say so. So, she said farewell and rose lightly
through the water.

The youngest mermaid swam to the surface
just after sunset, when the clouds were tinted
crimson and gold. A large ship stood still on
the calm sea, since there was not enough wind.
As night descended, the little mermaid heard
music coming from the ship and saw a hundred
coloured lanterns swaying in the mild breeze. She
swam close to the cabin windows. Occasionally,
as the waves lifted her up, she saw many well-
dressed people inside. The most beautiful of them
was a young prince with large black eyes. The
people were celebrating his twenty-first birthday.
After a while, the prince went to the deck, and the
sky lit up with dazzling fireworks. This startled
the little mermaid so much that she dived under
water. When she re-emerged, the stars seemed to
be falling down around her. The ship itself was
so brightly lit up that every single person was
visible. And how handsome the young
prince looked!

The little mermaid could not stop looking at the ship or the prince, although it was late and the party had ended. Even when the sea became restless, the little mermaid remained by the cabin window, rocking up and down on the water, looking in. Gradually, the winds picked up and the ship continued on its way. Soon, however, heavy clouds darkened the sky and lightning appeared in the distance—a fierce storm was approaching. The waves rose high, but the ship dived between them and then rose again on their foaming crests. The little mermaid was enjoying the weather but the sailors were not. After a while, the ship began to groan and finally the main-mast snapped and the ship lay on her side. The mermaid realized that the crew was in danger. She had to dodge the beams and planks of the wreck, which lay scattered on the water, but she was able to rescue the prince.

By morning, there was no sign of the storm or the ship. The rays of the rising sun brought back some colour to the prince's cheeks but his eyes stayed closed. The mermaid kissed his smooth forehead and stroked his wet hair. He seemed to her like the marble statue in her little garden. She kissed him again and wished that he might live. Soon, she caught sight of land. She saw great snow-capped mountains in the distance, green forests near the coast and close by, a large

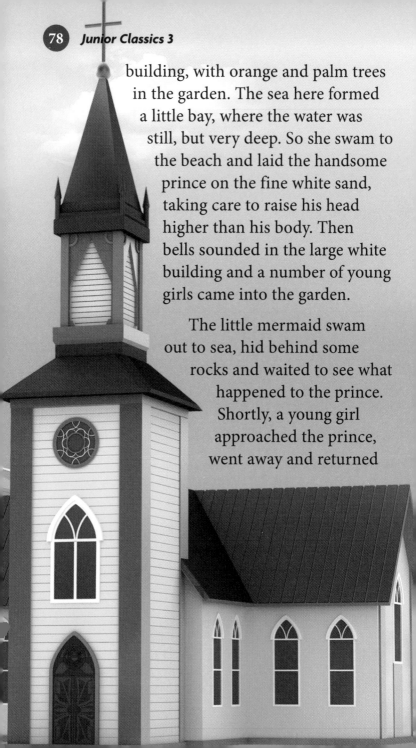

building, with orange and palm trees in the garden. The sea here formed a little bay, where the water was still, but very deep. So she swam to the beach and laid the handsome prince on the fine white sand, taking care to raise his head higher than his body. Then bells sounded in the large white building and a number of young girls came into the garden.

The little mermaid swam out to sea, hid behind some rocks and waited to see what happened to the prince. Shortly, a young girl approached the prince, went away and returned with a number of people. When the prince regained consciousness, he did not even look towards the little mermaid for he did not know she had saved him. When he was led away into the great building, she sorrowfully returned to her father's castle.

She often returned to the beach where she had left the prince but never saw him again. At first, she said nothing to her sisters, but kept getting sadder and sadder until all she did was wander in her garden, her arm draped over the statue that resembled the prince. Her flowers grew wild as she stopped tending to them and this gave the whole place a dark and gloomy look. Eventually, she told her sisters and they told two of their friends who knew who the prince was and where he came from and where he lived.

One day, the little mermaid's sisters took her to see the palace where the prince lived. It was made of bright yellow stone, with a long flight of marble steps, which ended right in the water. Through the windows, they could see grand rooms, with silk curtains, tapestries and beautiful paintings. In the centre of the largest hall, a fountain shot sparkling jets of water towards a domed glass ceiling. Now that she knew where he lived, the little mermaid spent many nights swimming quite close to the palace. As she got braver, she even went up the narrow channel under the marble balcony and sat in the shadows watching the prince, who thought he was alone in the bright moonlight.

While she was out at sea, the little mermaid often heard fishermen talking about the many good things the young prince was doing and was happy that she had saved his life.

The little mermaid remembered how she had saved him and how she had kissed him. However, the prince knew nothing of any of this. She grew fonder and fonder of humans, and wished she could explore their world, which seemed much larger than her own. Humans could travel by the seas, climb the highest mountains and own lands—woods and fields— that stretched far beyond what she could see. She had so many questions that her sisters could not answer, so she went to her old grandmother, who knew all about the upper world, which she called the lands above the sea.

'If humans do not drown,' asked the little mermaid, 'can they live forever? Do they never die?'

'Yes,' the old lady answered, 'they do die. In fact, their lifespan is much shorter than ours is. We sometimes live for three hundred years, but when we die, we turn into sea foam and then cease to exist.'

'Unlike us,' she went on, 'humans have a soul which lives forever, even after the body dies. It rises up through the air beyond the glittering stars. Just as we see the upper world when we rise out of the water, humans rise up to unknown and glorious regions which we shall never see.'

'Why don't we have an immortal soul?' the little mermaid asked her. 'I would give up the hundreds of years that I have to live, to be human for just one day, and to have the hope of knowing the happiness of that glorious world above the stars.'

'Don't say that!' her grandmother warned her. 'We are much happier and much better off than human beings.'

'If I die and turn into sea foam,' asked the little mermaid sadly, 'how will I hear the waves or see the pretty flowers or the sun? Is there anything I can do to win an immortal soul?'

'No,' her grandmother answered, 'not unless a man truly loves you and marries you. Then a part of his soul would glide into your body though this can never happen. Your fish's tail, which is so beautiful, is considered ugly on earth. They are so ignorant they think you need to have two legs, in order to be beautiful.'

Then the little mermaid sighed and looked sorrowfully at her fish's tail.

'Let us be happy,' said the old lady, 'enjoy the three hundred years we have to live, which is long enough, and then rest.'

That evening, the Sea King hosted a court ball, one of those splendid sights, which we can never see on earth. The crystal walls and ceiling of the large ballroom were lined with hundreds of colossal shells—some deep red, others grass green—with little blue fires in them, which shone through the walls, lighting up the sea.

Numerous fishes—purple and gold and silver—swam past and mermaids and mermen sang and danced in the broad stream that flowed through the hall. No one sang as sweetly as the little mermaid did. The whole court applauded her, and for a moment, she was very happy. However, she soon remembered her sorrows and crept from the party to sit in her garden alone.

Soon, she heard a bugle, a sign that the prince was sailing nearby. She decided to go and ask the sorceress, the sea witch, of whom she was normally terrified, for help in gaining the prince's heart and an immortal soul. She then set out on the deserted path that led to where the sorceress lived. She had never been that way before. There was nothing cheerful about the path, and the little mermaid had to pass the whirlpool, where the water twisted and turned like foaming windmills, crushing almost everything that came in its path.

The little mermaid swam through polyps with their ugly tentacles, past bits of ship wrecks and a mermaid who had been strangled by a polyp. This scared the princess so much that she almost turned back. But she remembered her purpose and regained her courage. She soon came to a

marshy ground, where fat water snakes rolled about. In the middle of all this, stood a house built from the bones of shipwrecked humans. There sat the sea witch, playing with the awful sea snakes.

'I know what you want,' the sea witch said, 'but it will only bring you sorrow, my pretty little princess. You want to replace your tail with a pair of legs so that the prince falls in love with you and you gain a soul. It is a stupid idea, but I will give it to you.'

Then the witch laughed loudly and disgustingly.

'You have come just in time, for after sunrise tomorrow, I would not have been able to help you for another year,' the sorceress continued.

'I will prepare a potion for you. Swim out to land before sunrise, sit on the beach and drink it. You will feel a great pain, as your tail shrinks into legs. People will call you beautiful and you will be the best dancer around. But every step you take will make you feel like you are walking barefoot on sharp knives. Are you willing to bear all that?'

'Yes, I am,' the princess answered.

'Are you sure? Once you turn into a human, you cannot ever be a mermaid again. And if the prince does not fall completely in love with you and marry you, you will not gain an immortal soul. If the prince marries someone else, your heart will break and you will turn into sea foam the very next day.'

'I will do it,' the princess said, turning pale.

'As payment for my potion, you must give me your sweet voice,' the witch said.

'But if you take my voice, what do I have left?'

'Your beauty, your graceful walk and your expressive eyes; surely these will help you charm your prince. Now, if you are brave enough, put out your tongue, so I can cut it off and put it into the potion.'

'I'll do it,' the princess said, and the witch prepared the potion.

She then gave the princess a vial filled with glittering potion.

The princess swam past her father's castle on her way to the surface, but she did not go in. Instead, she sneaked into the garden, took one flower from each of her sisters' flowerbeds and sent a thousand kisses towards the palace and rose up through the dark blue water, feeling like her heart would break.

The sun had not risen when the princess reached the stairs of the marble palace. As soon as she drank the potion, she felt like a sword was ripping her body apart. The pain was so intense she fell unconscious.

When she opened her eyes, the sun was shining and the handsome prince was by her side. She looked down and instead of a tail, she saw a pair of legs that ended in beautiful feet. However, she also realized she was naked. So she wrapped herself in her long thick hair.

The prince asked her who she was and where she came from but the mute mermaid could not answer him. She just looked at him sorrowfully with her deep blue eyes, hoping that he would recognize her. With every step, she felt like she was walking on needles, but she bore the pain and her graceful movements was as light as a soap bubble.

The princess was dressed in silks and satins and was easily the most beautiful creature in the palace. However, she was not very happy. Often, the slave girls would sing songs about the wonderful prince and his royal parents. The prince would clap and smile at the singing girls. During these times, the mermaid wished she had not traded away her voice. 'If only he could have heard me sing!' she thought to herself.

When the slaves danced, the mermaid danced with them. She danced like no one had ever danced before and soon enchanted everyone, including the prince. He called her his little foundling, and she danced for him often, ignoring the pain in her legs.

She slept on a velvet cushion outside the prince's bedroom. She went hunting with him, riding through sweet-smelling woods. They climbed to mountaintops— and although the mermaid's feet bled, she only laughed and followed him.

Late at night, when everyone was asleep, the mermaid sat on the marble steps, bathed her burning feet in the cold seawater and thought of her family.

One night, her sisters came up, singing sorrowfully. When she signalled to them, they recognized her and told her how much she had hurt them. After that, they came every night. Once, the little mermaid even saw her grandmother, who had not come to the surface in many years, and her father, the old Sea King.

As the days passed, the mermaid grew fonder of the prince, but he only loved her as one loves a child or a pet. Yet, unless he fell in love with her and married her, the mermaid would never gain an immortal soul. Moreover, she would turn into sea foam if he married someone else.

'Do you not love me?' the mermaid asked the prince with her eyes.

'You are so dear to me,' the prince said, apparently understanding her gesture, and added, 'for your heart is pure. You also remind me of a young woman whom I will never meet again. I was once in a shipwreck and the waves washed me upon the shore near a temple. The youngest temple maiden saved my life. I saw her only twice, and fell in love with her. But I cannot marry her since she is part of the temple. I am lucky that you were sent to me instead of her.'

'He does not know that I saved him,' the mermaid thought. 'I saw the pretty maiden he loves.' She sighed deeply but could not cry.

'She will not return to the world, so they will meet no more. But I will take care of him every day, love him and give my life for him.'

Very soon, the king and queen asked the prince to visit a neighbouring ruler, who had a very beautiful daughter. Everyone thought the prince would bring back his bride but the mermaid was not so sure.

'My parents want me to go but I cannot love her. She is not the temple maiden. If I were forced to marry, I would rather marry you, my dear little foundling,' the prince said, as he stood on the deck of a ship as the mermaid, played with her hair. She smiled, dreaming of human happiness and an immortal soul.

At night, when everyone was asleep, the mermaid sat gazing down through the clear water and thought she could spot her father's castle and see her grandmother with her silver crown. Her sisters swam near the ship at night looking pensive. The little mermaid tried to gesture that she was happy but suddenly a cabin boy appeared and her sisters dived under the water.

The next morning the ship sailed into the harbour of a beautiful town belonging to the king whom the prince was visiting. The church bells were ringing and soldiers lined the rocks through which they passed. Every day was a festival.

Soon, a week passed but the princess was nowhere to be seen. People said she was studying in a distant town, where priestesses were taught her royal virtues. When she finally arrived, even the little mermaid had to admit that she was very beautiful. Her skin was delicately fair and beneath her long dark eyelashes her smiling blue eyes shone with truth and purity.

'It was you,' the prince said. 'You saved my life that day on the beach.'

He folded his blushing would-be bride in his arms and turned to the mermaid.

'Oh! I'm so happy! My fondest hopes are all fulfilled now. I know you will be happy for me too.'

The mermaid kissed the prince's hand, but felt like her heart was tearing apart. She would die the morning after his wedding and turn into sea foam.

Soon, the church bells rang out and heralds rode about the town proclaiming the royal engagement a few days later, the two were married. The priests waved censers in which expensive perfumes were burning, and the bride and bridegroom joined their hands and received the bishop's blessings. The little mermaid wore a golden silk dress and held up the bride's train. Her ears heard nothing of the festive music, and her eyes did not see the holy ceremony. All she could think of was her impending death, and everything she had already lost. That evening, the newlyweds boarded the ship for their reception amid the cheering of the crowd. Cannons were roaring and flags were waving and a large tent had been erected for the festivities.

The ship, with swelling sails and a favourable wind, glided away smoothly and lightly over coloured lamps were lit, and the sailors danced merrily on the deck. The little mermaid was reminded of that night when she rose to the surface and saw the prince for the first time.

She knew this was the last day she would see the prince, the last time she would breathe the same air that prince for whom she had given up her family, her home, her voice and for whom she endured terrible pain every single day. It was also the last day she could gaze on the starry sky and the deep sea. She did not have a soul, and would never have one now. So she joined in the dancing and danced like she had never danced before. The pain cut through her intolerably but she did not stop dancing.

The celebrations ended long after midnight. The prince kissed his beautiful bride, while she played with his dark hair and arm-in-arm they retired to their cabin. Eventually, the little mermaid was the only one awake on the ship, apart from the helmsman. She leaned over the edge of the vessel, and watched for the first rays of the rising sun that would spell her doom.

She saw her sisters rising from the depths. Their long beautiful hair had been cut off.

'We've given our hair to the witch,' one of the sisters told her, 'so that we can save you. She gave us this knife. All you have to do is stab the prince before dawn. The blood you spill will cause your tail to grow again and you will be a mermaid again. That way, you will not turn into sea foam and will live out the rest of your years with us. Hurry! In a few minutes, the sun will rise and you might fail!'

Then they sighed deeply and mournfully and sank down beneath the waves.

The little mermaid drew back the prince's curtain and saw his wife sleeping with her head on his chest. She bent down and kissed his forehead and heard him mutter his wife's name in his sleep. She glanced at the reddening sky, then at the dagger, then back at the prince.

However, she hurled the knife as far as she could into the water. The water turned red, like blood, where the knife fell.

The little mermaid then turned once more, looked at the prince lovingly one last time and jumped overboard. She felt her body dissolving into sea foam even before she hit the water. The sun rose and in its warmth, she did not feel as if she were dying. She saw hundreds of beautiful transparent beings floating around her.

She soon realized her body was just like theirs and that she was rising higher and higher out of the foam.

'Where am I?' she asked, and her voice sounded ethereal, like the voices of those around her.

'Among the daughters of the air,' one of her companions said, 'a mermaid does not have an immortal soul, and relies on the love of a human being to gain one. The daughters of the air do not possess an eternal soul either, but we can gain one through our good deeds. For three hundred years, we cool the warm air that causes illness among humans, and carry perfume to flowers. Then, we receive an immortal soul and continue to bring happiness to humanity. You, my poor little mermaid, have suffered and endured. Your good deeds have raised you to the spirit world. Now, if you can continue doing this for another three hundred years, you may obtain an immortal soul.'

The little mermaid raised her eyes to the sky, and felt them, for the first time, filling with tears. On the ship, she saw the prince and his bride searching for her in the sea. They gazed sorrowfully at the foam, as if they knew what she had done. She floated to the prince, kissed the bride on her forehead and fanned the prince. Then, with the other daughters of the air, the little mermaid mounted a rosy cloud and floated off into the ether.

'So, in three hundred years, we will float into the kingdom of heaven?' she asked.

'We may even get there sooner,' one of her companions replied.

'Human children do not know this, but we can enter houses without being seen. Every time we see a child behaving well, we smile for we know a year has been cut from our test period. But when we see a naughty child, we shed tears of sorrow, and for every tear a day is added to our time of trial!'

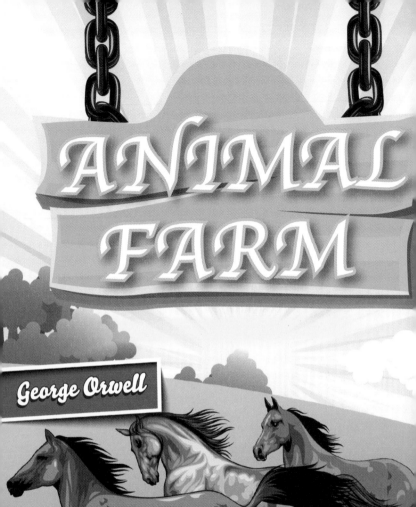

Mr Jones had shut the hen houses but, having drunk too much beer, had forgotten to lock the side doors. His lantern danced in his hand as he swayed in the yard of Manor Farm. He removed his boots, gulped down some more beer and headed up to his bedroom, where his wife was already asleep.

When the bedroom lights went off, there was a fluttering and stirring in all the buildings on the farm. Word had spread that Major, the prize Middle White boar, had had a strange dream the previous night and wanted to share it with the other animals. So a meeting was being held in the barn. Old Major was so well respected, that all the animals were willing to sacrifice their sleep to listen to him.

Major stood on a platform in the barn. He was twelve years old, quite stout and majestic. He had a wise and kindly look.

The animals of the farm streamed in and took up comfortable positions. The dogs, Bluebell, Jessie and Pincher, were followed by the pigs, who took a front row position in the straw. The hens preferred the window-sills, the pigeons sat on the rafters and the cows and sheep lay themselves on the ground behind the pigs. Clover and Boxer, the cart-horses, walked in together.

Clover was a well-built middle-aged mare while Boxer was a huge animal, and very strong. A white stripe ran across his nose giving him a rather stupid look. They were followed by the white goat, Muriel, and the donkey, Benjamin, the oldest of them all.

The ducklings filed in, and immediately fell asleep, while Molly, the vain and pretty mare

stepped in daintily chewing a sugar cube. The cat came last and quickly squeezed into the warmest spot. Only Moses the raven was absent, fast asleep on his perch in the backyard.

Old Major cleared his throat and began to speak:

'Comrades, you must know about my strange dream. I will talk about that later, now I want to say something else. Comrades, before I pass away, I feel duty bound to give you the wisdom I have learned in my long life.

'Comrades, we lead miserable and laborious lives. We get minimal food; we work to our full strength and once our usefulness is over, we are cruelly slaughtered! No animal is free in England or knows what leisure and happiness are. Animals' lives are miserable. In truth, we are just slaves.

'Is this because the land we live in is so poor that we can't be given decent lives? No! Our soil and climate are good; far more animals than those living here can be well fed. But we are not, because of Man, who is our greatest enemy. Remove Man from our lives and overwork and hunger will disappear!

'Also, even the miserable lives we lead are not allowed to reach their natural span. Our young piglets will be screaming for their lives in a year's time. All will come to that end: pigs, cows, sheep and hens.

'As for our dogs, an equally cruel fate awaits them!

'Comrades, it is clear that the evil in our lives is caused by Man's tyranny. If we rid ourselves of Man, our labour's produce becomes ours and we could become free and rich! Thus, we must work hard to overthrow the human race! That is the message I give to you! Rebellion! That's what we need. When it will come, I don't know, in one week or after a hundred years. But come it will!

'We must have perfect unity and comradeship for this struggle. Men are our enemies, animals our comrades!

'Remember this, comrades: whatever walks on two legs is our enemy; those that have wings or walk on four legs are our friends.

'We must never resemble Man and his ways. Thus, no animal should sleep in a human bed, live in a house, wear clothes, smoke tobacco, touch money, drink alcohol or trade in goods. All animals are brothers. We are all equal!'

Old Major then told the animals about his dream, which was a song his mother had taught him. Called Beasts of England, it talked of a golden future when Man will be overthrown, and England's fields will have only animals treading on them. Animals will be free of rings, harnesses, spurs and bits and will never again be beaten with whips. It also spoke of the good food they would all get. Old Major started to sing the song and the other animals soon began to sing along!

However, they were soon interrupted. The loud singing had awakened Mr Jones, who ran out thinking a fox had entered the premises. He fired some shots from his gun and the meeting quickly broke up and all the animals fled to their respective sleeping places.

A few weeks later, Old Major died peacefully and was buried at the foot of the orchard. A lot of secret activity went on in the three months after that. Major's speech had given the animals, the smart ones in particular, an entirely new direction in life. They felt it was their duty to be ready for the rebellion, whenever it came. Since the pigs were considered to be the most intelligent animals, the job of organizing and teaching the others fell to them.

The three most prominent pigs were young Napoleon, Snowball and Squealer. Napoleon was a huge Berkshire boar. He looked fierce and generally got his own way.

Inventive and quick in speech, Snowball was vivacious but did not have Napoleon's profound charisma. Twinkle-eyed Squealer had round cheeks, quick movements and a sharp voice. He was a talented orator and could be very persuasive.

These three pigs had detailed Old Major's ideas into a thought system which they called Animalism. Several nights, every week, they met in secret and explained the principles of this school of thought to the other animals. Initially, they were confronted with indifference and stupidity.

The raven Moses posed a bigger problem. He was Mr Jones's spy and he told the animals that there was a place called Sugarcandy Mountain high in the sky where all animals went after they died. There it was Sunday everyday and clover was available all the time, as well as linseed cake and lump sugar.

Not all the animals believed Moses, since he was a known liar;

but some did, and the pigs had a tough time persuading them that such a place did not exist. The meetings continued to be held in the barn and always ended with the singing of Beasts of England.

The rebellion happened faster and much more easily than any of the animals had expected.

Mr Jones had been a good farmer, but had fallen on bad days after losing money in a court case and began drinking much more than he was good for him. He would spend entire days in his chair, drinking and reading the news paper, sometimes feeding Moses pieces of bread that had been dipped in beer. Consequently, his workers became dishonest and idle, weeds choked his fields, the buildings' roofs remained unrepaired, the hedges were not cropped and, most importantly, the animals were not given their normal share of food.

On the eve of Midsummer Day in June, Mr Jones had gotten very drunk at a Red Lion pub and did not return to the farm until the next afternoon. The men milked the cows early and went out shooting rabbits. They did not bother to give the animals their food. As soon as Mr Jones got home, he went to sleep. The animals had stayed unfed till the evening.

They could not bear it anymore. A cow broke into the food shed. The other animals soon followed and all the animals began eating heartily. The noise woke Mr Jones up. He stormed into the shed with his men and whipped the animals. It was unplanned, but the hungry creatures struck back at their tormentors. The men were so scared that they ran for their lives and were soon flying down the road with the animals chasing them triumphantly!

Mrs Jones quickly packed her possessions and sneaked away through another route. Moses flew behind her, cawing loudly. The animals locked the main gate to the farm. Thus, before they even realized it, the revolution was over. Manor Farm was now theirs!

After galloping around the farm's boundaries, the animals rushed to the buildings and erased all traces of the Joneses' dreaded reign. They broke open the harness room and flung the nose-rings, the dog chains, the bits and knives, with which Mr Jones had castrated the lambs and pigs, into the well. Then they burnt the horses' halters,

reins, blinkers, whips and nosebags in to the rubbish fire which was burning the yard. Major had declared that all animals must go naked so Boxer flung his straw hat into the fire. Napoleon then gave the animals a treat of corn and biscuits for the dogs. They sang their song of rebellion and then went to sleep as they never had before.

The next morning, the animals surveyed all that was now theirs. They took a tour of the house, where they inspected the luxury in which the Joneses had lived. Molly took a piece of ribbon from the dressing table and was scolded for her foolishness. It was unanimously decided that the house would be preserved as a museum and no animal would live in it.

The pigs had learnt to read and write from a book belonging to the Joneses children. So, using pots of paint, Snowball grasped a brush in his trotter, deleted the name 'Manor Farm' from the main gate and painted 'Animal Farm' on it. Then, Snowball climbed up a ladder and painted the basic principles of Animalism—which would be the farm's new unalterable law—on a wall. The Seven Commandments were:

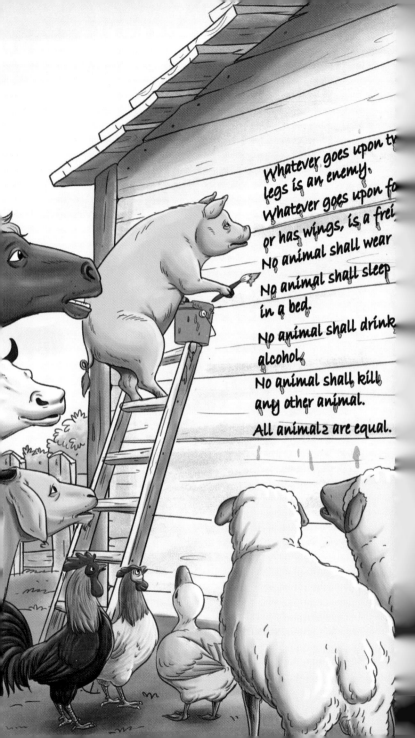

It was very neatly written, and except that 'friend' was written 'freind' and one of the 'S's' was the wrong way round, the spelling was correct all the way through. Snowball read it aloud for the benefit of the others. All the animals nodded in complete agreement, and the cleverer ones at once began to learn the Commandments by heart.

Just then, three cows started lowing loudly. They had not been milked for more than twenty-four hours and their udders were almost bursting. The pigs milked them and, soon, creamy milk filled up five buckets.

'What shall we do with the milk?' someone asked.

A hen said, 'Jones used to mix it with our food.' Napoleon stood in front of the buckets.

He said, 'Forget the milk. It will be taken care of. Now, the harvest is an important matter for us.'

The animals marched to commence harvesting. When they returned in the evening, the milk was gone!

The harvest was a tremendous success, though the pigs themselves did not really do any work. They supervized and directed the other animals. Their greater knowledge made them natural leaders. The other animals, including the hens and ducks, toiled all day and finally the harvest was done—two days faster than before.

The animals enjoyed every meal they ate, for it was the fruit of their labour. Boxer worked the hardest and earned everyone's admiration. Besides, the friendship among the animals was terrific. Nobody stole or grumbled about his rations. The fighting, jealousy and biting of the earlier days had disappeared.

Sunday was a 'no work' day and after breakfast a ceremony marking the rebellion was held. The flag—a green cloth on which was painted a horn and hoof in white colour—was hoisted and a general meeting was then held in the barn where the week's schedule was chalked out and resolutions were debated. But it was only the pigs who were allowed to introduce resolutions. Napoleon and Snowball were the most active and the two were always in disagreement. The rebellion song was always sung at the end of these meetings.

The pigs inscribed a new maxim on the barn wall above the Commandments in larger letters. It stated, 'Four legs good, two legs bad.' The sheep liked this maxim a lot. They would bleat it often when they were in the field.

Bluebell and Jessie meanwhile gave birth to nine puppies. As soon as they were weaned, Napoleon took over their care and kept them in a loft. The puppies were soon forgotten. The mystery of the milk was also cleared up. It was being mixed daily in the pigs' meals. The same was done with the apples. Some animals voiced their dissent and Squealer was sent in to explain matters.

'Comrades!' he declared, 'science has proven that milk and apples are good for the health of pigs. Many of us dislike apples and milk. I don't like them; but the farm's management depends on us.'

'So,' Squealer continued, 'we are eating the apples and drinking the milk for your sake! If we fail to do our duty, Jones will be back. Do you want that?'

All the other animals shook their heads. They did not want Jones back.

By the end of summer, the news of the revolution on Animal Farm had spread across the entire county. Napoleon and Snowball dispatched pigeons, instructing them to mingle with animals on nearby farms and tell them how the rebellion unfolded and teach them Beasts of England.

Mr Jones, drowning his sorrows in the Red Lion pub, complained to all who cared to listen to the story of the great injustice that had been meted out to him.

He got some sympathy from other farmers, but not much help.

At Foxwood and Pinchfield—the two farms adjoining Animal Farm—the owners, Pilkington and Frederick, respectively, were quite scared about the rebellion.

They naturally did not want their animals to learn about it and hated the very idea of animals running a farm. They spread rumours about fights, starvation and wickedness flourishing at Animal Farm. These tales were generally not believed. Instead, the talk of a lovely farm where animals were their own masters did the rounds. At some farms, bulls suddenly turned savage, sheep butted down hedges and ate the clover while cows kicked over the pails.

The rebellion song was known on all the farms. Farmers flogged any animal who sang the song but it continued to flourish among the animals and the birds.

One day in October, Jones and some other men tried to regain control of Animal Farm. Snowball had studied a book on Caesar's campaigns. Using those tactics, the animals effectively thwarted the men's efforts. All the animals played key roles in the battle.

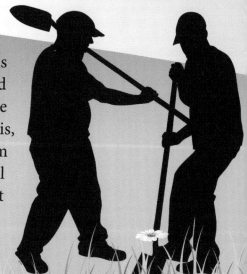

One sheep lost his life while Boxer killed a lad with his foot. He felt very sad about this, but Snowball told him not to get sentimental about it. Snowball got injured and was bleeding. His heroics earned him a gallantry award.

The sheep was given a formal funeral and a gallantry award. Mr Jones's gun, which lay in the mud, was set up at the foot of the flagstaff. The animals decided it would be fired twice a year, on 12 October, the day of the battle—now named the Battle of the Cowshed—and on the day of the rebellion, Midsummer Day.

Winter arrived and the earth became hard as a rock. These trying days were worsened by the disagreements between Snowball and Napoleon. While Snowball seemed to be full of ideas he learned from the books he read, Napoleon was good at getting support from the other animals as he disputed every one of Snowball's plans.

The sheep helped Napoleon in cutting short Snowball's schemes—the lambs would start bleating, 'Four legs fine; two legs terrible.' The noise they made pre-empted all discussion and soon became an effective strategy for Napoleon. Things came to a head when plans were made for the windmill.

Snowball felt that the knoll at one end of the farm was a good place to build a windmill, which could provide the farm with electricity so that the animals could have lights and warmth.

The windmill could also be used to power other electric implements beneficial to the animals. Snowball worked out all the plans for the windmill, greatly impressing the other animals— except Napoleon.

One day, surprisingly, Napoleon examined the plans, gave them deep thought and then urinated on them and walked away!

Gradually, deep divisions formed among the animals on the usefulness of the windmill.

Snowball agreed it would be difficult to build and would take time, but eventually the animals would have to only work three times a week. Napoleon held that increasing food production was a greater priority and they would starve if they wasted time building the windmill. Snowball spoke effectively about the great benefits of the windmill while Napoleon termed it 'utter nonsense'.

The animals were discussing the pros and cons of the windmill, when they heard loud baying. Nine huge dogs, wearing brass-studded collars, bounded into the barn. They went straight for Snowball, who sprang up and just escaped their fierce jaws. Snowball raced across the pasture and onto the road, while the dogs were snapping at him. He slipped and fell but got up and ran even faster as the dogs seem to gain on him. But Snowball finally managed to slip through a hedge and escape.

The animals were terrified and silenced. They quietly crept back to the barn and realized that these dogs were the puppies that Napoleon had taken from their mothers and reared in private. They saw that the dogs wagged their tails when Napoleon was around, just as the other dogs used to when Mr Jones was around.

Napoleon, followed by the dogs, next announced that there would be no more Sunday meetings. A committee, composed of pigs and headed by Napoleon, would decide all matters.

Squealer explained these arrangements to the rest.

'Comrades,' he said, 'I'm sure all animals here would appreciate comrade Napoleon's sacrifice in taking up extra labour. Leadership is a heavy responsibility.'

The animals were also quite surprised when Napoleon announced some days later that the windmill would be built. He told the animals to get ready for extra hard work.

In the evening, Squealer explained that Napoleon had never opposed the building of the windmill, and that Snowball's plan had been stolen from Napoleon.

In August, Napoleon announced that the animals would have to work on Sunday afternoons too. This was voluntary, but those who stayed absent would get half rations.

Construction of the windmill was a slow and lengthy process. Without Boxer, who seemed to be as strong as the others, nothing could have been accomplished.

Boxer toiled all day, but the shortage of material and food affected progress. No one knew how to get them. Then, one morning, Napoleon announced a new policy: they would begin trading with other farms, mainly to get the much-needed materials.

He also said that if extra money was required, they would sell eggs. The hens should welcome the sacrifice they were making towards the construction of the windmill.

The animals felt vaguely uneasy. Had they not made resolutions never to trade with humans and never to use money?

Napoleon added that they would not directly deal with humans. He had found a lawyer, Whymper, who would be the intermediary between them and the neighbouring farmers. The sly-looking Whymper visited every Monday. The animals avoided him but were proud to see Napoleon, on his four legs, giving orders to this man, a two-legged creature!

One day, the pigs decided to live in the farmhouse. Some of the other animals remembered a resolution that forbade animals from living in houses or sleeping in beds. Clover asked Muriel to read the commandment relating to this.

Muriel read, 'Animals will not sleep in beds with sheets.'

The pigs had 'updated' Old Major's commandment, but the other animals had not noticed.

In November, raging winds were followed by gale storms and the work on the windmill was stopped. What was worse was that one morning the animals woke up to see the windmill in ruins.

Napoleon immediately blamed Snowball for this.

'Comrades,' he said, 'Snowball has tried to avenge himself by destroying our year's work. I hereby sentence him to death. Any animal who captures Snowball will be well rewarded.'

The animals were stunned to learn that Snowball was guilty of such an act. They cried out in anger, and thought of ways to catch Snowball if he came back to the farm.

Right then, Snowball's footprints were seen near the knoll. Napoleon sniffed at them and announced that they were Snowball's. However, Snowball was never seen in the farm or elsewhere again.

There was an acute food shortage in January. Rations were reduced, and the animals were for some time forced to eat only roots and chaff. Starvation seemed to be round the corner. To conceal this fact from outsiders, Napoleon instructed the sheep to remark, in Whymper's presence, that their rations had been raised.

Also, Napoleon had the near-empty bins in the shed filled almost to the top with sand. Meal and grain was strewn over it and Whymper was given a glimpse of what seemed to be bins full of food.

One morning, Squealer told the hens that they would have to surrender all their eggs. Napoleon had struck a deal for 400 eggs a week. The money earned would help them get meal and grain till summer. The hens were terribly upset but could do nothing about it.

Meanwhile, Napoleon's relations with the other farmers became better. Now, in the yard, there was a heap of well-seasoned timber. Whymper told Napoleon to sell it, for both Frederick and Pilkington anxiously wanted to buy it. Napoleon hesitated, unable to decide who to sell it to.

Four days later, Napoleon ordered everyone to come to the yard. His nine dogs frisked around him and their growls terrified the other animals.

Napoleon then called upon the four pigs who had protested the abolishment of the Sunday meetings to confess their crimes. The pigs said that they had been in contact with Snowball, and had helped him destroy the windmill. They

had also made an agreement with Frederick to give him Animal Farm. When they finished their confession, the dogs promptly ripped out their throats. The hens, a goose and others made their confessions to various crimes and were summarily executed.

The other animals were thoroughly shaken. They didn't know what shocked them more: the animals' betrayal or the terrible payback they had just seen.

Then one morning Squealer, two dogs in tow, announced that Beasts of England would not be sung anymore. He said that it was no longer required as the rebellion was over.

Meanwhile, some animals remembered that one of their commandments stated that they must not kill their brothers. So Clover asked the donkey Benjamin to read out this commandment. Benjamin refused and Muriel was called to read it. The commandment now stated that animals shall not kill other animals without a cause.

Squealer or another pig now issued most of the orders. Napoleon did not come out as frequently as before. When he did, he was surrounded by his dogs, and a black cockerel, who crowed each time before Napoleon made a speech. Napoleon was referred to as 'Our Leader' or 'Comrade Napoleon', 'Protector of All Animals' and other titles that the pigs created for him.

One day, three hens made a startling confession that inspired by Snowball, they had joined a plot to assassinate Napoleon. They were killed on the spot and Napoleon was guarded even more carefully.

Four dogs stood by Napoleon's bed at night, and a pig tasted his food first, to make sure he was not poisoned.

Eventually, the windmill was completed and the animals admired their masterpiece, uttering triumphant cries when it started functioning. Napoleon inspected the windmill and promptly named it 'Napoleon Mill'.

The timber was sold to Frederick. The farmer had wanted to settle accounts with a cheque, but Napoleon insisted on cash and wanted it to be paid before the wood exchanged hands. The money was adequate to purchase equipment for the windmill. Napoleon gave the animals a chance to inspect the cash. But three days later Whymper came rushing into the farm to meet Napoleon. There was a loud cry of anguish. The notes were fake!

Worse, Frederick and his men attacked the farm soon after, leading to a very bloody battle.

The tragedy of it all was that the humans used explosives to completely destroy the windmill.

Fifteen armed men killed a number of animals. Napoleon himself got shot in the tail. Squealer, who appeared only after the battle ended, called it a 'victory', for—in the end—the human beings were chased away from the farm, thanks to Napoleon's ferocious dogs.

Some days later, the pigs found some whisky in the farm's cellars. That night, the other animals could hear loud singing from the house. Napoleon was wearing one of Mr Jones's old hats.

Late the next morning, Squealer appeared, looking very dejected, and announced that Napoleon was dying. The animals had tears in their eyes. A little while later, Squealer came out again to announce that anyone caught drinking alcohol would be punished with death.

The next morning, however, Squealer told the animals that Napoleon was recovering.

After a few days Muriel saw that there was another commandment that they had remembered incorrectly. This one actually read: 'Animals shall not consume alcohol to excess.'

The animals began to rebuild the windmill. Boxer had injured his hoof badly, but continued to work hard. He told Clover that his lungs too were giving him trouble. As another winter set in, life became harder. However, Squealer convinced them that it was still better than it had been under Mr Jones. The animals agreed. There were more marches, more ceremonies and more celebrations and the animals enjoyed them all.

In April, Animal Farm became a republic, and Napoleon was unanimously elected its first president.

Then, one evening in summer, Boxer fell down and could not get up. Soon, Squealer came out and announced that arrangements were being made to take Boxer to the hospital. Two days later, a van showed up. As the animals rushed to say goodbye to Boxer, Muriel read the words on the van. 'Horse Slaughterer…Hides and Bone-Meal Dealers,' it said.

'Boxer is being taken to the butcher!'

The animals cried, 'Boxer get out.'

But the van had gathered speed, and was soon far away from them. Squealer announced three days later that Boxer was dead.

'I was at his side till the end,' he said as he wiped a tear away from his eyes. He added that the van had once belonged to the slaughterer but the veterinary surgeon had bought it and not yet changed the name.

The animals were very relieved when they heard this.

As the years passed many animals died and were replaced by others. Napoleon now weighed more than 150 kg and Squealer had become so fat he could hardly see! Old Benjamin was the same, only a bit greyer around the muzzle.

The farm had become more prosperous but the windmill was not being used for electrical power. Instead, it was used to mill corn, which fetched big money.

There were no luxuries for the animals. In Animalism, declared Napoleon, the greatest happiness was in working strenuously and living meagrely. Only the pigs and the dogs, it seemed, had become prosperous.

One day, Clover neighed loudly! She had seen a terrifying sight: it was a pig walking on his hind legs! It was Squealer. Sometime later came a long line of pigs walking on one leg.

Then came Napoleon. He stood by himself majestically, on one leg, casting haughty glances all around. In his trotter he held a whip.

The animals were terrified and amazed. Huddling together, they silently watched the pigs marching in the yard. Their world had turned on its head.

Then, the sheep started bleating loudly, 'Four legs are good but two are better!' And they kept on repeating their tune.

Benjamin read the writing on the wall: 'All animals are equal but some are more equal than the rest.'

Soon after, Napoleon strolled in the garden smoking a pipe and wearing a black coat, breeches and leggings made of leather. His beloved sow donned a silk dress.

The next week, dog-carts drove into the farm. Neighbouring farmers had been invited to an assessment tour of Animal Farm. They admired all they saw. The animals did not know who to fear more—man or pig.

In the evening, loud laughter and noises of merry-making emanated from the farm house. The animals, led by Clover, crept to the house and the taller ones looked inside. Half a dozen eminent pigs and an equal number of farmers sat at the table. Napoleon occupied the place of honour. The pigs were totally at ease sitting in chairs. They had been having fun playing cards and broke off to gulp down a toast.

Pilkington said he was greatly satisfied with Animal Farm. A lengthy period of misunderstanding and mistrust had ended.

He said the orderliness and discipline here was a good example to other farmers. He noted that the lesser animals here got least food and did more work compared to any farm creatures in the county.

Napoleon, after saying that the farm was a cooperative enterprise of the pigs, stated that it would no more be called 'Animal Farm' but by its original name 'The Manor Farm'.

There was hearty cheering and beer mugs were drained.

Suddenly the animals who were watching the scene from outside, noticed strange happenings in the room. Some of the pigs had four chins, some five and others three. There was chaos inside and a quarrel erupted. There were suspicious glances, loud shouting, table-banging and sharp denials. It seemed that Mr Pilkington and Napoleon had both played the ace of spades at the same time.

Twelve voices howled in anger, all sounding alike. And as the animals looked on, the pigs' faces had changed. The animals outside looked from man to pig and pig to man, again and again. But now it was impossible to state which face belonged to whom.

Other Titles
In The Series